Baby Is Sleeping

Storyline **Matthew Pacer**
Illustrations **Steven Butler**

Baby mouse is sleeping.

Mother mouse is sleeping.

Baby dog is sleeping.

Mother dog is sleeping.

Baby lamb is sleeping.

Mother lamb is sleeping.

Baby donkey is sleeping.

Mother donkey is sleeping.

Baby cow is sleeping.

Mother cow is sleeping.

Baby camel is sleeping.

Mother camel is sleeping.

Baby Jesus is sleeping.

Mother Mary is sleeping.

Everyone is sleeping.